Special thanks to Tabitha Jones

For Alexander Jones

ORCHARD BOOKS

First published in Great Britain in 2019 by The Watts Publishing Group

1 3 5 7 9 10 8 6 4 2

Text © 2019 Beast Quest Limited
Cover and inside illustrations by Dynamo
© Beast Quest Limited 2019

Team Hero is a registered trademark in the European Union
Series created by Beast Quest Limited, London

A CIP catalogue record for this book is available from the British Library.

ISBN 978 1 40835 562 6

Printed in Great Britain

The paper and board used in this book are made from wood from responsible sources.

Orchard Books
An imprint of Hachette Children's Group
Part of The Watts Publishing Group Limited
Carmelite House, 50 Victoria Embankment, London EC4Y 0DZ

An Hachette UK Company
www.hachette.co.uk
www.hachettechildrens.co.uk

AN ARMY AWAKENS

ADAM BLADE

ORCHARD

MEET TEAM HERO ...

JACK

POWER: Super-strength
LIKES: Ventura City FC
DISLIKES: Bullies

RUBY

POWER: Fire vision

LIKES: Comic books

DISLIKES: Small spaces

DANNY

POWER: Super-hearing, able to generate sonic blasts

LIKES: Pizza

DISLIKES: Thunder

CONTENTS

"IT IS done, Supreme Commander," the Agent said, bowing his head. "I now have all three compass pieces." As he gave the news, the Agent couldn't help smiling beneath his mask. He had recovered the final compass piece from right under the noses of Team Hero. But, as he watched the grey, half-mummified face on the holoscreen before him, this sense of triumph drained away. The Supreme Commander's stony, milk-white stare seemed to bore into him, and, though the sun baked down on the skyscraper roof where the Agent stood, he suddenly felt cold.

"I have everything needed to find and awaken the Hidden Army, Master," he said, unable to keep his voice from trembling. As the Agent waited for a reaction from his master's scarred and wizened face, his knees began to shake.

Finally, the Supreme Commander's bloodless lips parted, revealing rotting, blackened teeth. "And the young Heroes?" he asked, his voice a grating hiss full of menace.

"Unfortunately, they are still alive," the Agent said. He hadn't meant to go on, but found himself blurting out everything, his babbling voice no longer under his control: "They have prevented me from entering my cruiser ... But that is only a minor inconvenience. I have my jet-boots, and I have the compass. Team Hero can't stop me awakening the army now. And once its thousands of Soldiers are activated, nothing will stand in my way." Under the Supreme

Commander's cold, unblinking stare,

the Agent's voice faltered. "I mean,

your way ..."

"Do not fail," the Supreme Commander hissed. Then, without warning, the holoscreen flickered and disappeared, leaving the Agent staring at a metal grate covering a vast air conditioning pipe. But as he turned away to gaze out over the city of Baotecca, he couldn't shake the horrible creeping feeling that those milky blue-white eyes still watched him, seeing everything and judging his every move ...

CHAPTER 1

TRAPPED!

"WHAT A mess," Jack said, gazing around what was left of the sculpture garden of the Baotecca Museum. Jagged pieces of the museum's stone brickwork stuck up from the well-tended grass. Several sculptures had been flattened beneath fallen masonry.

At the centre of the wreckage hovered the Agent's base, a shining metal platform about the size of Jack's family's apartment in Ventura City — but Jack had seen it transform into many different shapes, even an aircraft. Ruby walked around the base, her orange eyes narrowing with interest as she inspected its strange devices and screens, all flashing with lights. The structure gave off an electrical static that set Jack's teeth on edge.

He and his friends had managed to capture the base, but only after the Agent's henchman, Fade, had stolen the final compass piece from the museum vault. Now the compass was complete, it could lead the Agent to a powerful mechanical army.

"What do we do?" Danny asked.

"We need to work out where the Agent's taking the compass, then stop him waking up the Hidden Army and destroying the world." Jack said.

Ruby turned away from the base, one eyebrow raised. "As plans go, that's pretty weak on detail," she said.

"Maybe Chancellor Rex will have an idea of where to go next. Hawk?" Jack said, speaking to his Oracle, "can you patch me in to Hero Academy?"

But as Hawk began to reply, the clatter of booted feet made Jack turn. A stout, red-faced security guard, dressed in the blue uniform of the museum, burst into the sculpture garden.

"Thank goodness you're still here," he panted. "We have an emergency in the vaults."

Jack's pulse quickened. "What's happened?" he asked.

The security guard wiped the sweat from his forehead. "That thief — Fade — collapsed part of the vault's ceiling. Some of our researchers got trapped inside, and it sounds as if the rest of the ceiling could give way any minute."

"Lead the way," Jack said, already heading towards the museum door with Ruby and Danny at his side.

The security guard jogged ahead of them through the deserted café, guiding them down a wide corridor lined with broken exhibit cases then into the museum's main hall. Jack drew his sword, Blaze, and Danny lifted his crossbow as they picked their way across their earlier battleground, which museum employees were now trying to clean up.

They hurried onwards down a marble staircase and through more passages until finally the guard turned into a service corridor with strip lights overhead. "Down there," he wheezed, pointing to a narrow staircase on the other side of a thick security door.

Jack led Ruby and Danny down the stairs. At the bottom, he found an underground room with a high, domed ceiling. A huge pile of stone, bricks and metal struts blocked an archway that led to the next chamber. Jack could just make out the sound of muffled cries, almost drowned out by another, far more ominous noise — the creak and groan of stone and metal stressed to breaking point.

"I could blast the rubble away..." Ruby said, her orange eyes glimmering.

"Inadvisable," Jack's Oracle said into his ear. *"The structure is extremely unstable."*

"Hawk says not to," Jack said. "If we had time, we could prop up the arch with something — but I don't trust that ceiling to hold another minute. I think I'll have to shift it bit by bit."

Jack flexed his scaled hands, feeling a warm tingle as power flowed into his palms. Then he ran his eyes over the slabs of stone and plaster that blocked the entrance. He noticed several wide cracks running through the carved lintel of the arch itself. He took a deep breath, suddenly reminded of a game he used to play when he was small — take the wrong block and it all comes tumbling down. *Well, here goes ...*

"Keep well back!" he shouted to the people trapped on the other side of the debris. "I'm going to get you out."

Jack started at the top of the pile, carefully sliding a section of stone away. *CREAK!* Jack froze, hardly breathing as dust trickled from above. When nothing else happened, he

carefully set the stone down.

Jack edged another slab from the pile. *CRACK!* Chips of plaster pattered down. A deep groan, like metal wrenching out of shape, echoed through the passageway.

"That doesn't sound good," Danny said.

"All the more reason to get those people out fast," Ruby said. In the tense silence that followed, Jack set about moving the rest of the rubble. Each new section of brickwork or stone he shifted caused more creaking and groaning from above — but the ceiling held. *For now ...*

Jack worked steadily, his nerves thrumming. Eventually, he'd opened a gap big enough to see into the next room. A group of men and women crowded together against a glass-fronted cabinet a short distance away, their eyes wide with fear. But the gap was still too small for anyone to fit through. A massive section of stone blocked the way.

"Don't move!" Jack told the trapped researchers. He wedged the fingers of his scaled hands beneath the stone, letting the warmth in his hands grow as the super-strength built. Then he heaved upwards, grunting with effort

as his arms took up the strain. A long, grating creak sent shivers of alarm up Jack's spine. *Oh no ...* Fear jolted through his body as a terrible *CRACK!* rang out from above.

"Ruby, Danny — get under here!" he cried. As his friends leapt to his side, Jack heaved the huge slab of stone above their heads like a shield. An instant later, a rumble like an earthquake filled the passage as the doorway, and the ceiling above it, came crashing down.

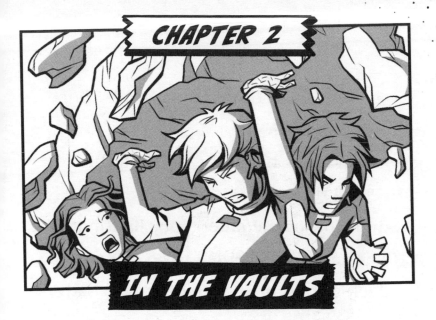

CHAPTER 2

IN THE VAULTS

JACK BRACED his body as tonnes
of stone and brick thundered on to
the slab he was holding up. Ruby and
Danny crouched at his side as more
masonry tumbled down. The floor
beneath them seemed to shudder.
Choking dust filled Jack's lungs.
He could hear panicked yells and

screams from the vaults ahead. *I hope everyone's OK ...*

Amid the chaos, the bulbs in the ceiling flickered out, leaving only the dull glow of the emergency lighting. The rumbling seemed to go on and on. Jack gritted his teeth, his whole body shuddering as he strained to keep the wreckage from crushing him and his friends. *I don't know how much longer I can keep this up ...*

Finally, the booms quietened to a gentle patter, until there was only silence. Jack could taste the dry grittiness of stone dust between his teeth. All his muscles burned.

"Is everyone all right?" Danny asked.

"I'm OK," Ruby said, her voice sounding small in the sudden quiet.

"Me too," the security guard croaked from the back of the basement room.

Jack heard muttering from the dusty gloom ahead.

"We're all OK back here," a woman called out. "Just cuts and bruises, I think." Jack felt a rush of relief despite his trembling muscles.

"Jack?" Ruby asked. "Are you OK?"

"Not exactly ..." he grunted. "I need to put this stuff down, but that might set off another collapse. Can everyone get to safety?"

"We're on it," Ruby said. A pair of bright rays slanted past him as Ruby and Danny switched on their torches.

Trying to ignore the burning pain in his arms and core, Jack stood tall, sweat trickling down his face and dust tickling his nose. *Don't sneeze!* he told himself over and over as Ruby and Danny led people out of the vault.

When the last woman finally limped past to follow the security guard up the staircase. Jack let out a sigh of relief. *We did it!*

"Keep well back," he told Ruby and Danny. Then he bent his knees and leaned forwards, letting the huge weight of brick and stone slide from his arms and across the floor. He tensed as the echoes of the crash died away, expecting another collapse at any moment. But when he looked up, he could see every wire, fitting and girder exposed in the dark ceiling space above him. There was no more stone left to fall.

Jack let his aching muscles relax. Through the archway ahead, he could see the glass-fronted cabinet the researchers had been crouching against. One of the panels had been smashed, and inside, he could just make out stone tablets carrying what looked like the now familiar markings of the Taah Lu — the ancient civilisation that had fought the Agent's people and hidden the compass pieces.

"That must be where Fade found the compass piece," Jack said, pointing. He stepped through the archway and headed towards the artefacts. Other metal objects remained inside the cabinet — all clearly of Taah Lu origin. Ruby and Danny arrived at Jack's side as he reached a row of strange metal spears. Their tips were much thicker than normal spears, like metal cones.

Ruby gingerly removed one of the spears. Despite its age, it looked almost new and stood about a metre taller than her.

"Hey," Danny said. "Isn't that like

the spears the Taah Lu used to fight the Hidden Army?"

"I think you're right," Jack said. "Hawk, can you bring up an image?"

Jack's visor shimmered then cleared, displaying a hologram of a wall carving they'd found in an abandoned Taah Lu city. Jack and his friends had discovered the mural very close to the remains of a disassembled Soldier of the Hidden Army. The bottom of the carving showed a battle scene. Huge mechanical Soldiers were laying waste to a city while the Taah Lu fought back with long spears. And now Jack could see that each spear had the same, heavy cone-like tip as the spear Ruby now held.

Jack drew another spear from the cabinet. It felt strangely light considering its size, and not cold like ordinary metal did. "They're a pretty odd design," he said. "I wonder if there is something special about them."

"The metal they are constructed from does not match any in my databases," Hawk's voice said in Jack's ear. *"It has certain properties similar to Xanthrum."*

"I think we should take some with us," Jack told the others. "Hawk says the metal's a bit like the Xanthrum the Agent makes his weapons from —

which means we might be able to use them against him."

"I don't know ..." Danny said. "I seem to remember the guards being pretty insistent that we didn't remove the exhibits from the museum."

Jack smiled. "That was before we saved them and all the museum visitors from the Agent and his grenades, remember? Still, you do have a point. And I don't think we'll be able to sneak these out, either."

Suddenly, Ruby yelped in surprise. Jack glanced over to see the spear in her hand disappearing into itself with a *swoosh*. It stopped shrinking at about the length of Ruby's forearm. She held it up, grinning.

"It'll be much easier to get these past security now," she said. "Just push the little button near the end of the shaft." She turned the metal cylinder over, showing Jack and Danny a tiny button. Jack quickly found a switch on his own spear and shrank it with a *swish*.

Jack hid the spear inside the sleeve of his combat suit. Ruby and Danny did the same. As they turned to leave, Jack's earpiece crackled.

"Ruby, Danny, Jack — can you hear me?" Professor Yokata said, speaking through their Oracles.

"I read you, Professor," Jack said, quickly echoed by Ruby and Danny.

"Our satellites have tracked a strange and powerful energy signal heading for the coast from your

current location," Yokata said. "Do you three know what's going on?"

Jack's stomach twisted. "I'm afraid so," he said. "The Agent managed to get hold of the final compass piece and escaped using his jet-boots. I'm guessing that the energy signature is the compass, and he's using it to find the Hidden Army. But at least now we know where he's headed."

"We'll track the signal," Yokata said, "and I'll ask Chancellor Rex to dispatch a team immediately, but it will be some time before they arrive."

Ruby grinned, her orange eyes gleaming. "I've got an idea," she said.

CHAPTER 3

OCEAN SKIRMISH

BACK IN the garden, Jack and his friends circled the Agent's metal base.

"So, you actually think you can fly this thing?" Danny asked, quirking an eyebrow at Ruby.

"Only one way to find out," she said, then stepped up on to the platform. Danny followed, then Jack, feeling the strange vibration of the metal beneath his feet. Ruby walked over to a high-backed metal chair near the centre of the platform. She sat down and shuffled backwards in the massive seat, her feet dangling above the floor. Then she frowned down at the keypad on the armrest.

"This shouldn't be too hard," she said. "There are only a few buttons …"

Ruby jabbed at the keypad. The craft gave a gentle shudder, the metal floor panels folding up around them, quickly overlapping each other to form four walls and a roof. Soft blue lighting filtered down from the ceiling, and a small metal table rose up from the floor. Ruby yelped as a robotic arm shot from a compartment in her armrest and plonked a slender metal goblet in front of her. Another arm slapped a plate of what looked like dead beetles down before Ruby. Jack grimaced. *Smells like rotting cabbage!*

"Eww! Wrong button!" Ruby said. "That must be what the Agent eats!" She pressed another key, and with the same gentle whir, the table vanished back into the floor, taking the stinking meal with it. The panels overhead shimmered and rearranged themselves again, settling into the teardrop shape of a cockpit. A steering column rose up before Ruby as blue-tinted windows appeared around them. Through the glass, Jack saw how the base had nimbly tapered into a sleek, V-shaped wing.

"That's more like it!" Ruby said, tugging the steering yoke. *WHOOSH!*

The craft took off with a burst of speed that snatched Jack off his feet and slammed him into the back wall.

"Ouch!" Danny cried, pinned to the wall beside him.

Through the front window, Jack could see Baotecca's skyscrapers speeding past as they climbed steeply.

"Slow down!" Jack yelled.

Pushed back in her chair by the craft's acceleration, Ruby stretched to reach the controls. "I'm trying!" she cried. Finally, she managed to grab the yoke again and eased it forwards.

Jack sighed with relief, starting to relax ... until he spotted a skyscraper dead ahead. "Watch out!" he cried.

Ruby tugged at the steering. The craft lurched sideways, missing the skyscraper but throwing Danny and Jack across the cockpit. They landed on top of each other in a heap.

"Wish this thing had seatbelts," Danny grumbled, rubbing his elbow as Ruby righted the craft.

Jack untangled himself from Danny, struggling to his feet and crossing the metal floor to stand behind Ruby's chair, holding tightly to the back. Danny followed suit.

"Hawk, can you show me the compass's energy signal?" Jack asked his Oracle. "Send it to Kestrel too, so Ruby can see."

"Certainly," Hawk said.

An image materialised on Jack's visor. He recognised the coastline. A glowing blue X flashed a little way out to sea — but it seemed to be moving in circles. Another X appeared, shooting across the map at astonishing speed. *That's us*, Jack realised.

"Hold on tight!" Ruby said. She barely moved the steering yoke, but Jack felt himself tugged sharply sideways.

"Wah!" Danny cried, losing his grip. Jack shot out a hand and grabbed Danny's arm, pulling him back to the chair. On Jack's visor, the second X headed after the first.

"This is a piece of cake!" Ruby said. "We'll catch the Agent up in no time!"

Peering through the tinted windscreen of the craft, Jack saw white-capped waves ahead of them and realised she was right. *We've travelled miles in just a few seconds!*

"Hey! Look," Danny cried, pointing through the cockpit's windshield. "Isn't that the Agent?" Jack followed the line of his finger to see a slender figure clad in shining silver flying in circles low over the water ahead.

"Let's get a closer look," Ruby said. Jack's stomach gave a lurch as she angled the craft downwards towards the Agent. As they neared his circling figure, Ruby eased back on the thrusters and levelled the craft, frowning. "You're right," she said. "I wonder what he's doing."

"It doesn't look like he's raising an

army," Jack said. "Maybe we're not too late to get the compass piece back." But at that moment, the Agent looked up, the dark eye sockets of his mask locking on to the craft. Twin blasts of fire shot from his jet-boots and he zoomed over the waves towards them.

THUD! The sound of metal hitting metal echoed through the cabin. A hideous wrenching sound came from one side, and Jack looked up to see a panel peeling back, showing a patch of sky, and then the Agent's masked face.

"How dare you steal my cruiser!" the Agent growled. His gauntleted hands hooked around the edge of the hole, and he started to pull himself through.

"Ruby, keep the craft steady. I'm going to get the compass!" Jack leapt, swiping his sword at the Agent's masked face. The Agent drew back his head, and Jack clamped his free hand around the side of the gap in the hull and used his super-strength to pull himself through.

Stumbling to a crouch on the speeding craft's wing, Jack gasped at the sudden rush of air. The Agent stood before him, wielding a blaster.

"Get off my cruiser!" the Agent shouted, sending a hail of blaster fire. Jack rolled sideways, feeling the metal

beneath him judder as the blaster-fire struck. He flipped to his feet, staggering for balance as the wind buffeted against him.

The Agent snatched a Xanthrum grenade from a compartment in his suit and lobbed it. Jack scrambled back out of its path just as it exploded, lifting him off his feet.

"Oof!" He landed on his back so hard, his teeth clashed together. When he looked up, he saw smoke pouring from a new hole blasted in the side of the cruiser. The craft listed sideways suddenly, making his stomach lurch. Jack struggled up. He could hear the bleep of alarms coming from inside.

"Are you OK in there?" Jack cried.

"We're fine, but I think that grenade hit something important!" Ruby yelled.

The Agent prowled towards Jack, blaster raised. Before he could fire,

Jack leapt, driving a flying kick into his enemy's chest. The Agent hurtled backwards, landing on his back with a metallic clang. His blaster spun from his grip and skittered away, dropping down to the ocean. Jack leapt forward, straddling the Agent's chest with his legs. Then he lifted Blaze.

"Give me the compass!" Jack shouted, grabbing the Agent's metal mask where it covered his throat.

"Never!" the Agent cried, arching his back, struggling to get free. The craft pitched sharply, knocking Jack back, and the Agent's mask came with him. It flew from his hand as he slid by the blast hole made by the grenade.

"Gah!" Jack just managed to catch hold of the rim of scorched metal. He clung for his life and looked up to see the Agent without his mask for the first time. Jack's gut clenched in horror at the sight. A blue-green pockmarked shell covered the top part of the Agent's massive, misshapen skull, but the whole bottom half of his face looked like it had been peeled apart. The red muscle and gums of his wide, lipless mouth were clearly visible. Jack could see rows and rows of curved yellow fangs surrounded by four protruding

tusks. The man's eyes bulged from dark sockets, bloodshot and yellow with dark vertical slits for pupils. *So that's his true face!*

Still holding tight to the torn structure of the roof, Jack swallowed his rising panic as the Agent crawled towards him along the wing. His bulbous eyes blazed with fury and saliva dripped from his curved teeth. Jack tightened his grip on Blaze. Suddenly, the whole craft tipped so violently that his arm was almost wrenched from its socket. Power surged through his scaled hand as he clung desperately to the metal, dangling by one arm above the waves. With a furious cry, the Agent tumbled past him off the now vertical craft, and plunged into the ocean after his mask, sending up a plume of spray as he vanished from sight.

Before Jack could see whether his

enemy re-emerged, the craft slammed upright again, smashing his body against the metal panels. He let out a shuddering breath of relief. Then he hauled himself through the blast hole left by the grenade.

Jack landed in a crouch in the smoke-filled cabin below. The calm blue lighting had changed to pulsating red, and a chorus of alarms beeped from several places at once.

"How are we doing?" Jack asked Ruby and Danny. Both were holding the steering yoke, which shook wildly as they struggled to keep it straight.

"What does it look like?" Ruby said

through gritted teeth. "Whatever keeps this thing steady seems to have stopped working. I'd say a bunch of other parts are damaged too."

"And the Agent?" Danny asked.

"He fell into the water, taking the compass with him," Jack said. "I don't know if he survived. That metal suit has to be pretty heavy."

"So, does that mean we won?" Danny asked. But before Jack could answer, all the lights in the craft flicked off at once. Suddenly Jack's stomach dropped away as he was thrown back towards the roof.

"We're going down!" Ruby cried.

CHAPTER 4

FROM THE DEEP

IN THE darkness and chaos of the falling craft, someone's knee caught Jack in the gut. He fell back to the floor, winded and bruised, feeling water rushing up all around him.

"Hawk, torch!" he managed to wheeze. His headlamp flickered on, and he saw that water now gushed up through the blast hole in the craft.

"We have to get out of here," Ruby said. She and Danny were getting to their feet, as the steadily rising churn of water lapped at their knees.

"Surely there must be a door," Danny said.

"If there is, it's electric," Ruby told him. "And the power's dead."

"Then I'll just have to tear a way out!" Jack said. Half wading, half swimming, he crossed to the smooth overlapping panels of the nearest wall, aiming a punch at the seam between two plates. *CLANK!* His fist made only a tiny dent, and Jack realised with alarm that the water had already almost reached his chest. Fear gripping hold of him, he drew back his scaled fist and slammed it into the metal again. This time a small crack appeared, more water spraying through, adding to the flood that inched up his body. *We're going to drown!*

"I'll burn a way out," Ruby said, focussing her eyes on the ceiling. Twin beams of fire hit the metal and started to trace a line. But the water poured as fast as ever. *She'll never get us out in time!*

"Hurry!" Danny cried, his chin

barely above the water.

Jack clenched his fist again, ready to aim another hopeless punch. But at that moment, the craft came to a stop with a loud, metallic clang. A heartbeat later, Jack felt a buoyant, lifting sensation, and the water level around him started to drop.

"We're saved!" Danny cried, grinning as the water drained away.

Despite his relief, Jack couldn't help frowning. "But how?" he asked.

Danny cocked his head to listen. His bat-like ears twitched. "From the echoes," he said, "it sounds like we collided with something enormous, and it's now lifting us upwards."

"Well, I'd still like to get out of here," Ruby said.

"Agreed," Jack said. As the last of the water drained away, he peered through the blast hole in the craft's side and gasped. Sunlit water spilled away to reveal that they were on a colossal metal structure pushing up through the ocean's surface.

Beckoning for his friends to follow him, Jack stepped out on to a vast rising platform, just as it slowed to a halt.

"Whoa!" Danny breathed. They stood together, side by side, water

dripping from their sodden clothes as they looked about. The Agent's cruiser was at the centre of a huge oval metal structure with pointed towers climbing into the sky all around the edge. Shimmering, electric-blue lines ran in complex patterns over the surface of the metal, like the veins on a leaf. Something about the smooth angles and gleaming metal reminded Jack of the Agent's tech.

"I've got a bad feeling about this place," he said.

"Look how huge it is!" Danny breathed.

"Three point eight kilometres across

at the widest point, to be precise,"
Hawk's voice said in Jack's ear.

"It looks like a fortress of some kind," Ruby said, gazing at the gleaming pillars on the far side of the structure. "Those pointed buildings must be defence towers. This has to be where the Hidden Army is. The Agent must have somehow raised it up from the sea."

"But I can't see any sign of him now," Jack said. "I guess we'll have to keep our eyes peeled."

They strode across the vast metal expanse, stepping carefully over the shimmering blue seams, until they reached the closest of the metal towers. As they drew near, Jack spotted narrow windows far above them. *But no door.*

He circled the tower and noticed something strange. The shape of a six-fingered hand was engraved into the metal of the tower, at roughly the height of his head.

"Six fingers, like the Agent!" Jack said. "This place must have been made by his people."

"But how do we get in?" Ruby asked.

"Isn't it obvious?" Danny said. Before anyone could stop him, he reached out and placed his palm inside the six-fingered imprint.

"AAARGH!" Danny cried, his hand sinking into the shining metal wall, which now suddenly rippled like water, sucking in his arm up to the armpit. Jack grabbed Danny by the other wrist and pulled. "OW! You're going to pull my arm off!" Danny screamed, his eyes wide with panic.

The wall's made of some kind of Xanthrum! Jack realised.

Still gripping Danny tightly with one arm, Jack drew Blaze and slashed at the metal, but it was like slicing through jelly. The blade passed

straight through, the edges of the cut
closing back together instantly. Danny
groaned in agony.

"I've an idea!" Ruby said. She drew

the Taah Lu spear from her sleeve. As
she pressed its button, it extended out
fully. Ruby drew it back and struck
at the wall near Danny's arm.

This time the metal parted around
the spear point, making a funnel
shaped hole. *No ...* thought Jack a
moment later ... *the spear is somehow
absorbing the metal!* But it wasn't
getting Danny out!

"Help!" Danny cried. The wall still
tugged at Danny, but less roughly
than before. Ruby drew the spear
out of the shimmering, liquid metal.
Jack saw that its tip now glowed a
dim blue. The wall of metal seemed

shallower than it had been.

"Any other ideas?" Ruby said. Jack's mind raced as Danny's face contorted with pain.

"Only one," Jack said, "but you're not going to like it."

"What?" Ruby asked.

"Take a breath and close your eyes." Then he grabbed Ruby's hand and, still holding tight to Danny, hurled himself and his friends into the wall.

As the viscous metal closed around him, Jack felt intense pressure squeezing his body, like being deep under water. *Maybe this wasn't such a good idea ...* But the wall was now

only a few centimetres thick and his
momentum carried him and his friends
through to the
other side.

They'd made it
inside, but there
was no time to
congratulate
themselves. The
blare of an alarm
shook through
Jack, as purple
lights flashed on
and off all around
them. They were

in a bare, circular lobby made from

the same metal as the outside of the fortress. Jack glanced about, expecting an attack — but the place seemed deserted. A staircase spiralled upwards, running around the tower walls all the way to the top. A second, shorter staircase led downwards.

"Everyone OK?" Jack asked his friends.

Danny grimaced, putting his hands over his ears. "I'm just about all in one piece, but that alarm's making my brain hurt."

They started down the metal staircase. It opened on to a long corridor that curved away ahead of them. Purple holoscreens hung in the air overhead every few metres along the passage, each one showing a printed message in a strange text which flashed in time with the constant alarm. But, before they had gotten halfway down the passage, the alarm stopped, and the screens all changed at once to show the Agent's masked face.

Jack froze, staring at the repeated images, shuddering as he remembered what lay beneath the mask's silver surface. Ruby and Danny both stopped beside him as the Agent started speaking.

"You have made a grave error following me here," the Agent said. His deep voice echoed along the corridor. "It will be your last mistake. Five thousand years ago, when my people were still members of the High Command, we created this place. The compass led me here, to my people's ancient fortress." The Agent's voice rose in triumphant glee: "The compass has unlocked the power at its heart. Now I am master of the Hidden Army. Long ago, my people intended to use this army to destroy the human race. But, after only one measly victory over the Taah Lu, weaklings among

79

my own ancestors changed their minds because they were so troubled by the deaths of worthless surface dwellers. They abandoned their invincible army of automatons and pledged never to raise arms again. The fools! I will succeed where they failed. I will destroy each of your pathetic cities until none remains. The Supreme Commander will reward me greatly for my efforts! And you three … ? You will perish!"

With that final word, the screens all vanished at once, leaving only a purple glow lighting the passage.

"The Supreme Commander?" Danny

said, eyes wide. "That's really bad, right?"

"Yep," Jack said, feeling suddenly cold. "Even General Gore was afraid of him. Which means we have to stop the Agent waking up the army at any cost. Let's go."

Brandishing Blaze, Jack led the way along the curved passage, every nerve in his body thrumming. At any moment, he expected the Agent or a Soldier to leap out and attack. But instead, the passage carried on and on with no doorways, curving gently as it sloped downwards. The further they travelled in the silent gloom, the more uneasy Jack felt. *The Agent has to be in here somewhere*, he thought. At last, Danny let out a frustrated growl and turned, hands on hips.

"We've been walking for miles," he said. "We must be going in circles."

"No," Ruby answered. "The walls are curving more the further we go — that means we're spiralling inwards."

Jack gazed at the passage ahead, seeing how it now curved more sharply than before. "I think you're right," Jack said. "But towards what?"

Danny shuddered. "Only one way to find out, I guess."

The three friends continued

onwards until they rounded a bend and found themselves suddenly at the tunnel's end. They stopped, staring at the immense space ahead.

An oval chamber, bigger than any stadium Jack had seen, opened before them. A platform ran around the edge of the chamber, surrounding an enormous hole easily as big as three football pitches. Dozens more levels, both above and below, skirted around the central void, all held up by massive metal columns. Jack shook his head, horror creeping over him as he gazed about the huge space. Every level was packed with ranks of immobile, giant hulking Soldiers, hunched forward and covered in interlocking gold and silver plates.

"Now we know what fully intact Soldiers look like," Danny said,

gaping. Each Soldier stood around twelve metres tall, with four roughly humanoid arms all brandishing a variety of deadly-looking weapons.

Jack spotted saws, scythes, whips and knives ... He swallowed hard. "There must be hundreds of Soldiers on each floor," he said. "Which means thousands all together."

"Maybe hundreds of thousands ..." Ruby said.

A blue light flashed from deep within the pit. Jack cautiously stepped to the edge and peered over.

Perhaps twenty floors down, he could see something small that pulsed with a faint light.

"Zoom in, please, Hawk," he asked his Oracle. Jack's visor shimmered, and the view resolved to show a bright disc, spinning in the air, emitting pale blue light.

"The compass!" he said, pointing.

Danny peered down at Jack's side. "It looks like it's getting brighter the faster it spins," he said.

Ruby nodded and pressed her Oracle to her ear. "Kestrel says the compass is somehow powering this whole complex. Its energy level is increasing steadily. When it reaches full power, I'm guessing these Soldiers will all wake up."

Danny ran his eyes over the endless tiers of automatons and let out a shaky breath. "Then, we need to destroy it, and quickly," he said.

Jack nodded. "But how do we reach it?"

A throbbing sound made Jack leap back, just as the Agent shot from a behind a Soldier and zoomed upwards, powered by his jet-boots. He stopped to hover before them above the chasm.

"I've been waiting for you!" he cried. "Now I shall show my people the glory of conquest." The Agent lifted his gauntlet, bringing his other hand over to the button below his knuckles.

No! Jack's whole body tensed, as if making to charge at his enemy — but he knew it was no good. He would not be able to cover the distance in time.

The Agent pushed the button, sending three gleaming jets of Xanthrum from his wrist. Each shimmering arc of metal hit one of the colossal Soldiers nearest to them. At the heart of each Soldier, between curved armour plates, a fist-sized sphere glowed a bright blue as the Xanthrum filled it. Jack watched in horror as cogs and wheels beneath

the Soldiers' metal casing whirred and
spun. Then, with a hideous buzzing
hum, the three Soldiers turned
towards Jack, Ruby and Danny, their
gleaming weapons raised.

CHAPTER 5

THE BATTLE BEGINS

"WHAT'S THE plan, guys?" Danny said, lifting his crossbow.

"We fight!" Ruby answered. Before the nearest Soldier could reach them, she shot streams of fire from her eyes. The flames glanced off the Soldier's metal armour without leaving a mark.

Jack leapt towards the second

Soldier, who swung a spiked mace on a chain. Using all his strength, Jack cut the mace free. It spun away, hitting a column with a clang, but the Soldier rotated, slicing for Jack with a circular saw attached to a different arm. Gripping Blaze in both hands, Jack hacked at the saw again.

He saw Danny fire an energy bolt at the third Soldier, but it bounced harmlessly off the curved metal shell.

This is hopeless! Jack thought as he landed another mighty blow, this time almost severing the Soldier's saw. *Only Blaze can even make a dent! Unless ...* Jack suddenly remembered how Ruby's spear had sucked in the Xanthrum from the wall. Maybe there was another option ... But before he could draw his own spear, his robotic opponent suddenly attacked again.

Jack leapt out of range. The Soldier hovered closer, and Jack stepped back, his heels hitting the column behind him. The scythe cut through the air in a shimmering arc. Jack ducked, hearing metal hit metal above his head with a hideous screech. A tortured, wrenching groan sent a jolt of terror though his gut. He dived sideways just as part of the colossal metal column came crashing down, right on top of the droid. Jack leapt to his feet to see the Soldier's body crushed by the column, its whirring limbs still spinning their weapons.

One down, two to go.

Jack turned to see Ruby circling her opponent, her jaw clenched as she sent two steady streams of fire towards it, forcing it back. But as Jack watched, Ruby's flames suddenly fizzled out. Her shoulders slumped with exhaustion. "I can't keep this up!" she cried.

"Use your spear!" Jack said.

But the Soldier was already lunging towards her, slicing for her with a long, shining blade. Adrenaline filling him with strength, Jack threw himself before his friend. Focussing all his power into his hands, he sent Blaze whistling down, hacking at the Soldier's wrist, severing the weapon. The blade hit the ground with a clunk, but immediately, the wrist shimmered and a new weapon formed from the cut metal — a long, pulsing drill.

As Jack chopped at the drill arm, Ruby sent her spear jabbing past him through a gap between two of the Soldier's metal plates. When the spear hit the glowing ball at the heart of the Soldier, its tip started to glow brightly as it sucked the Xanthrum in.

The Soldier made a sputtering, choking sound, and Jack noticed its movements slow, the cogs and gears inside growing sluggish.

"It's working!" Ruby cried. Jack lifted Blaze, grunting with effort as he brought it down and — *clang!* — he chopped the Soldier's entire arm off.

"Regenerate that!" he said.

Jack glanced towards Danny nearby, to see him keeping the third Soldier at bay by firing energy bolt after energy bolt from his crossbow.

"Use the spear to draw off the Xanthrum at the heart of the Soldiers

like Ruby is doing!" Jack called.

Danny nodded at his bow. "My hands are full at the moment," he said.

"I'm coming," Jack called. But then, from the corner of his eye he saw a

long metal whip swipe toward Ruby.
Jack turned and swung Blaze, hacking
at the deadly coil. It almost tugged
Jack from his feet. But just then Ruby
gave her spear one final twist in the
Soldier's heart. The Solider sputtered
as its whip unwrapped itself from
Jack's sword. Its heart turned dark
and its internal cogs chugged to a halt.

Two down!

"Now I really could do with a third
hand!" Danny called. As Jack turned,
he saw his friend using his crossbow
like a shield, fending off a scythe, while
jabbing his spear between the Soldier's
armour plates, striking the heart and

absorbing its Xanthrum. The spear tip glowed brighter as it drew in the energy. Glancing at Ruby's spear, Jack saw it thrumming with power, almost too bright to look at directly.

"Hawk," he gasped. "What's happening? Will the spears explode?"

"Unlikely," Hawk said, *"but they seem to have limited capacity. I forecast that when they reach full capacity, they will cease to draw the Xanthrum from the Soldiers' hearts."*

Jack leapt to Danny's side and drew his own spear, opening it with a *swoosh*. Ruby joined them an instant later. As Jack attacked, the

Soldier spun, slicing a curved scythe at his face. Jack used Blaze to parry the strike, seeing a glimpse of Ruby catching a blow with her mirror shield, while Danny once again thrust his spear into the Soldier's glowing heart. Jack followed suit. They both held their spears steady, side by side, drawing its Xanthrum away. At last, the mechanical Soldier fell to the ground with a thud that echoed through the vast chamber.

As Danny, Ruby and Jack stood together, gasping for breath, Jack noticed all their spear tips now glowed white. *They're full!* he realised.

"Finally!" The Agent's voice echoed up from the void, sending a shock of dread through Jack. He glanced over to see that the shining blue light of the compass had become a bright sphere of energy, filling most of the chasm. The Agent hovered beside it, lifting his arm with a triumphant cry.

"While you were busy fighting," the Agent called, "the compass reached full power! You might have Taah Lu spears, but they can't help you now!"

Jack watched as blue Xanthrum jetted from the Agent's wrist guard, hitting the compass. The glowing disc started to transform, opening like a geometric flower with hundreds of petals. Its pulsing blue light grew so bright Jack had to narrow his eyes.

Still more Xanthrum flowed from the Agent's gauntlet. The compass spun faster and faster and a sound like a roaring wind filled the chamber, and everything started to shake.

"Get out of here ..." Jack told Ruby and Danny. "Now!"

"But what are you going to do?" Ruby asked.

"The only thing I can do," Jack cried. "Stop that maniac!"

Before Ruby could argue, he turned and leapt off the balcony.

CHAPTER 6

THE ARMY AWAKENS

SPEED AND terror snatched the breath from Jack's throat as he plummeted towards the sphere of pulsing energy many storeys below. He could feel electric static crackling in the air around him, sending shocks across his skin. Buffeted by air currents that filled the void, he used his aerial training to dive for the Agent.

I've only got one chance at this!

He hurtled down past levels crowded with thousands of ranked Soldiers, his eyes tearing from the shockwaves of energy that emanated from the compass.

The Agent looked up when Jack was only a dozen metres above him.

"No!" the villain shouted.

BOOF! Jack's shoulder slammed into the villain's metal suit. He grabbed the Agent's arm. Locked together, they spun through the air. The void was narrower here and they crashed on to a level not far from the compass. As they

hit, Jack lost his grip on the Agent's armour and tumbled across the metal floor with bone-jarring force.

Winded and dazed, he shook his head to clear his dizziness. The sound of rushing wind suddenly died. Everything fell still. In the silence, a low hum started up, coming from the compass but quickly spreading. Soon the whole chamber seemed to vibrate with an electric buzz. Jack watched in horror as bright blue streams of Xanthrum shot from each spike on the compass, branching as they sped through the room, jetting into every last corner of the vast space. Whirrs and clicks sounded from the thousands of Soldiers as bright Xanthrum filled the energy cores at their hearts.

"You're too late!" the Agent cried. "My army is awakening!"

But, with his eyes fixed on the

glowing compass, Jack suddenly had an idea. *Blaze can damage the Soldiers... So, maybe, just maybe ...*

Jack leapt to his feet and lunged towards the edge of the void, Blaze held ready. But before he could reach it, he felt a metal claw clamp shut around his waist, stopping him in his tracks. He craned his neck to see that a spherical Soldier held him fast in its robotic hand. From all around him, he could hear the sound of gears and electric saws whirring to life. *They're awake!*

Jack felt the claw around his chest tighten, squeezing the breath from his body and crushing his ribs. Fear and adrenaline burned through his veins. *One ... last ... shot ...* With all his super-strength, he drew back his hand and hurled his sword directly at the glowing compass.

Please! Jack thought, his ribs screaming with agony as he watched his blade slice through the air. *Please work ...*

CLANG! Blaze hit the glowing sphere and lodged there. The compass kept spinning, as fast as ever. Jack's heart sank.

So much for that ...

But then the compass seemed

to stutter, sparks flying as its spin suddenly reversed. The chamber flashed light and dark in time with the compass's erratic pulse. It started spinning faster and faster, out of control ... Then it burst apart. Jack threw up his arms to shield his face as fragments of scalding metal pattered down. A series of booms echoed through the chamber as all the activated Soldiers dropped to the floor.

Then there was silence.

Jack felt the claw around his waist open, letting him go. He let out a sigh of relief as his ribs settled back into place, then he turned to face his enemy.

The Agent stood frozen, staring at the void where the compass had been. When he turned to face Jack, the eyes behind his mask darted about as if looking for an escape route.

"You've failed," Jack said. "The army will never harm anyone again." He heard the Agent swallow hard, then his armour rattled as he started to shake.

"Maybe it's over for me," the Agent hissed, the pure venom of hate in his quivering voice. "But for you, it's only begun. Nothing will stop him. He is coming."

Despite his victory, Jack felt a chill run over his skin. He knew exactly who the Agent meant ... *The Supreme Commander.* An enemy more dangerous than any the surface world had ever faced before.

Suddenly a shaft of amber light shone past Jack. The Agent threw up his hands, shielding his eyes. Jack turned to see a glowing door hanging in the air, just above the platform. A tall silhouette moved through the strange entrance. A moment later, a slender figure in a long white robe strode through, followed by two more. Each had the same insectoid face and toothy mouth as the Agent, and Jack leapt back, fear coursing through him. But

something about the calm bearing of
the beings, and the gentleness in their
round, bulbous eyes made him stop in
wonder.

"Peace to you," one of the creatures said, bowing its head. "We owe you our thanks."

"Who are you?" Jack managed, though his throat felt dry as sand.

"I am Leena," the creature said in a low female voice. "And we are known as the Dremayn." She spread her hands, encompassing the beings on either side of her. "The one you know as the Agent is one of our people ... and he has broken every rule in our realm. We did not know what he had planned until the compass pieces were reunited. We came as quickly as we could. Many generations ago, our people fell under the thrall of the Supreme Commander and embraced war. We almost made ourselves monsters in our thirst for conquest. But when our ruler walked through the ruins of a devasted Taah Lu city, she truly understood the horrors of war. From that point on, our people pledged never to raise arms again." Her wide eyes narrowed as she turned to the Agent. "Since then all of us except one have kept our ancestors' pledge ..." She turned back to Jack, her expression serious. "We are impressed by your powers, young heroes, but hope you will also resist the temptation to use them for your own gain at the expense of others."

Jack lowered his own head. "Team Hero only uses its powers for good," he said.

"Then you will go far," Leena said, her lipless mouth spreading in what Jack thought might have been a smile. Then she turned her bulging eyes on the Agent. He stood gazing at the floor, his shoulders sagging.

"Come," she said, gesturing towards the portal. "You must stand trial for your crimes." The Agent didn't move at first, but when the two other white-robed Dremayn crossed to take an arm each to lead him away, he put up no resistance. Before following the Agent into the portal, Leena lifted a hand. A pure white light shone from her palm, spreading to form a bright sphere. As the white sphere widened, fragments of blue metal hovered up from where they lay, then floated towards her from all over the chamber. The fragments settled gently in her palm. *The broken compass!* Jack realised.

"You have done what the Dremayn could not do," Leena said. "For that, you have our gratitude. The compass and its army will never trouble your people again." The white light faded, and then she raised her other hand

in farewell to Jack and disappeared through the door.

As the amber portal vanished, Jack heard a clatter of footsteps, and turned to see Danny and Ruby hurrying towards him.

"We followed the balcony around and found some stairs," Ruby said.

"That was a seriously good throw!" Danny told Jack. "I really thought for a moment there that the Agent was going to win."

"It'll take more than a crazed homicidal maniac with his own mechanical robot army to get the better of Team Hero!" Ruby said.

Jack grinned. "Too right. Evil is going to have to try a bit harder if they want to conquer this world."

But then a cold finger traced his spine as he remembered the last words the Agent had said to him. *The Supreme Commander is coming ...* Jack thought. *Evil will try again — it always does. I only hope we're ready for the final battle when he arrives.*

THE END

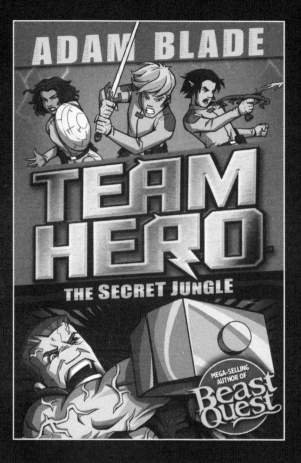

READ THE FIRST BOOK IN
SERIES 4:

THE SECRET JUNGLE

CHAPTER 1

INTO THE JUNGLE

IN THE Hero Academy Command
Centre, the main monitor had been
playing Dr Jabari's message on
loop for the last ten minutes. Jack
watched carefully, while also keeping
an eye on his friend Ruby. Danny
had an arm around her shoulders.
Though she was obviously upset,

her eyes glinted with determination. Jack's heart ached for her. He knew what it was like to see your parents in danger.

Also standing before the bank of terminals and screens were Chancellor Rex, the Academy's head, and their tutors Professor Rufus and Professor Yokata. All of them looked deeply concerned.

Ruby slammed a hand on the control panel, pausing the footage.

"We've got to do something!" she said.

Professor Yokata nodded gravely. "And we will, Ruby," she said.

"Though we have to know what we're dealing with first."

"Where is this Taah Lu temple Dr Jabari was investigating?" asked Jack.

"The Parracudo Jungle," said Chancellor Rex. "One of the last great wildernesses on our planet. The Taah Lu were an ancient civilisation who stood against the High Command's attacks."

Check out THE SECRET JUNGLE to find out what happens next!

IN EVERY BOOK OF
TEAM HERO SERIES
FOUR there is a special
Power Token. Collect
all four tokens to get
an exclusive Team Hero
Club pack. The pack
contains everything you and
your friends need to form your
very own Team Hero Club.

FREE
TEAM HERO
CLUB PACK

MEMBERSHIP CARDS · MEMBERSHIP CERTIFICATE
· STICKERS · POWER GAME · BOOKMARKS

Just fill in the form below, send it in with your four tokens
and we'll send you your Team Hero Club Pack.

SEND TO: Team Hero Club Pack Offer, Hachette Children's Books,
Marketing Department, Carmelite House, 50 Victoria Embankment,
London, EC4Y 0DZ.

CLOSING DATE: 31st December 2019

WWW.TEAMHEROBOOKS.CO.UK

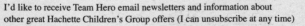

Please complete using capital letters *(UK and Republic of Ireland residents only)*

FIRST NAME
SURNAME
DATE OF BIRTH
ADDRESS LINE 1
ADDRESS LINE 2
ADDRESS LINE 3
POSTCODE
PARENT OR GUARDIAN'S EMAIL

I'd like to receive Team Hero email newsletters and information about
other great Hachette Children's Group offers (I can unsubscribe at any time)

*Terms and conditions apply. For full terms and conditions please go to
teamherobooks.co.uk/terms*

*TEAM HERO Club packs
available while stocks last.
Terms and conditions apply.*